The
Runaway
ave

Stories linking with the History
National Curriculum Key Stage 2.

Fife Council Education Department

King's Road Primary School

King's Crescent, Rosyth KY11 2RS

First published in 1998 by Franklin Watts

This paperback edition published in 1999

Franklin Watts
96 Leonard Street
London EC2A 4RH

Franklin Watts Australia
14 Mars Road
Lane Cove
NSW 2066

Editor: Matthew Parselle
Series editor: Paula Borton
Designer: Kirstie Billingham
Consultant: Dr Anne Millard, BA Hons, Dip Ed, PhD

A CIP catalogue record for this book
is available from the British Library.

ISBN   0 7496 3456 1 (pbk)
       0 7496 3093 0 (hbk)

Dewey Classification 305.5

Printed in Great Britain

The Runaway Slave

by
Andrew Matthews
Illustrations by Martin Remphry

W
FRANKLIN WATTS
NEW YORK•LONDON•SYDNEY

AM I NOT A MAIN AND A BROTHER ?

1

A Bundle of Old Clothes

Toby hurried along the crowded street.
At four o'clock his master, Mr Tomlinson,
had sent him to Adams Mews to deliver a
watch to Mr Bishop. Toby had been given
strict instructions to give the watch to Mr
Bishop in person, but Mr Bishop had not

been at home. Toby had waited for him for
an hour and a half. Now evening had fallen
and the streetlights were lit. Mr Tomlinson
was expecting Toby to help with the
shutting of the shop, and Toby was worried
that he might be late. Mr Tomlinson would
not punish him for lateness, or even scold
him, but he had a way of looking at Toby
that made Toby feel he had let his master
down, and he hated to do that.

Toby was small and thin, with curly ginger hair that no amount of brushing could flatten. He had blue eyes and a freckled face. He had been abandoned as a baby, and brought up in a Foundling Hospital where he had been taught how to read, write and learn off-by-heart long passages from the Bible that he did not really understand. On his twelfth birthday, Toby had been apprenticed to Mr Tomlinson, who owned a jeweller's shop in Pickett Place, and it had been the luckiest day of his life.

Mr Tomlinson was a kindly man, who believed that it was his duty to help those worse off than himself. He never beat Toby or starved him, the way that some other masters did to their apprentices – though he did insist that Toby went to church twice on Sundays. Toby did not mind the hymn-singing, but sometimes the sermons went on for so long that he found it difficult to stay awake. But apart from Sundays, Toby could not wish for a better master.

There were so many people in the street that Toby could not help bumping into them, and he lost count of the number of times he said, 'Beg pardon!'

At last he came
to a side-street, and
he paused on the
corner to think for a
moment. If he turned
off the main road he
would have further
to walk, but there
would be no crowd
to hold him up and
he would stand a
better chance of being on time.

The street was narrow. On either side
of it, tall houses leaned towards one
another like gossips whispering secrets.
Some of the householders had hung out
lamps and others had not, so that Toby
walked from pools of light into pools of
shadow. The street smelled of smoke and
sewage, and the cobbled road was dotted

with small heaps of horse-droppings. Toby
ignored the smells as best he could, and
breathed in through his mouth.

He was half-way down the street when
he saw something up ahead, just at the
edge of a patch of light. It looked like a
bundle of old clothes that had been
dumped at the side of the road. Toby began
to walk round the bundle, and as he did so
it moved and groaned. A hand stretched
out into the light, a brown-skinned hand
with fingers
crooked as if to
grab the hem of
Toby's coat.

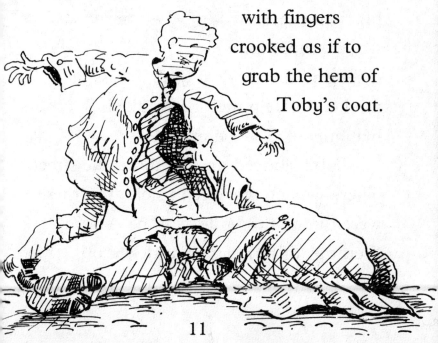

Toby stepped back, stared down and a face looked up at him.

It was a man's face. At first, Toby thought that the man must be deformed, but then he saw dried blood on the man's top lip, and realised that he was injured. His left eye was closed by bruised, puffy flesh, his right eye was no more than a slit and there was a gash across his forehead. 'Help me!' he croaked. 'Please help me, in God's name!'

Toby glanced up and down the street. There was no one else in sight, but there were too many shadows to be certain. 'Perhaps this man was attacked by footpads,' he thought. 'They could be hiding in the dark, waiting to attack anybody who stops to help him!'

Toby frowned. What should he do? What would Mr Tomlinson tell him to do?

In his mind, Toby seemed to hear Mr Tomlinson's voice saying, 'Never turn away from those in need. We must do as Jesus told us, and care for the poor and sick.'

Toby did not know if the man was poor – though he had never heard of a rich black man – but he was in need all right. He looked too badly hurt to stand.

'I'll bring help,' Toby said. 'I'll be back
as quickly as I can!'

Then he broke into a run.

2

Property

Mr Tomlinson and his manservant George were closing the shutters outside the shop when Toby arrived.

'Mr Tomlinson!' Toby panted. 'I was coming back – and there's a man – and – !'

'Calm yourself, Toby,' said

Mr Tomlinson. 'Gather your thoughts and start again.'

Toby explained what had happened as clearly as he could. Mr Tomlinson listened patiently, then said, 'Think carefully, Toby. Are you sure the man is hurt?

Perhaps he drank too much at a tavern.'

'He didn't smell of drink, sir, and he had blood on his face,' said Toby.

'Then lead me to him,' Mr Tomlinson said briskly. 'George, you had better come with us.'

The man was still lying where Toby found him. He was barely conscious. 'Help me, someone!' he moaned.

'Be easy in your mind, good fellow,' said Mr Tomlinson. 'You are among friends.'

The man started at the sound of Mr Tomlinson's voice. He opened his eyes wide in terror. 'Don't send me back!' he begged. 'Don't send me back to Mr Lisle!'

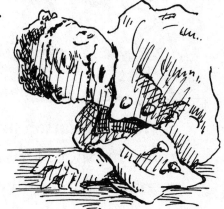

'I mean only to take you to my house,' said Mr Tomlinson. 'George, help me get him to his feet. Toby, fetch Dr Sharp. Tell him the matter is urgent.'

Mr Tomlinson lived in the rooms above his shop. Dr Sharp rode there in his carriage. Toby sat beside the driver, who

cracked his whip and bellowed, 'Make way there!' as they rocked and rattled along. Toby had never ridden a fast-moving carriage before and he clutched the seat tightly, certain that he would be thrown off and crack his head open on the cobbles, but at last they arrived safely at Pickett Place.

The man was downstairs, in the small room behind the shop where Toby slept.

Dr Sharp loosened the man's clothing and examined him. 'He has three broken ribs and he may be bleeding internally,' he said grimly. 'I shall take him to Saint Bartholemew's hospital immediately.'

'I shall come with you,' said Mr Tomlinson.

'Please, sir, may I come too?' Toby said.

'You have done enough,' Mr Tomlinson

replied. 'Tell cook to leave out bread and cold meat for my supper. I may be gone some time.'

Mr Tomlinson did not return until past ten o' clock, and he was surprised to find Toby waiting for him, half-asleep in a chair beside the fire in the back parlour.

'You should have been in bed long ago,' Mr Tomlinson said.

Toby yawned and rubbed his eyes. 'I wanted to know about the man,' he said.

'He is in the hands of the surgeons,' said Mr Tomlinson. 'He would certainly have died tonight if you had not found him. All we can do now is pray.'

'Who is he, Mr Tomlinson?' asked Toby. 'Who beat him?'

'His name is Jonathan Strong, and he is a slave,' Mr Tomlinson said. 'He was beaten by his master, Mr Lisle, who threw him out into the street and left him for dead.'

Toby noticed an angry light in Mr Tomlinson's eyes. 'Will Mr Lisle be arrested?' he said.

Mr Tomlinson sighed. 'He is a lawyer, and knows the law. Jonathan Strong has no money and a dark skin. Such people cannot expect justice from a magistrate's court. In the eyes of the law, slaves are property, like pieces of furniture, and slave-owners may do with them just as they wish.'

Toby frowned. 'But... I thought...' he said.

'You thought what?' said Mr Tomlinson.

'Aren't all people supposed to be equal in the eyes of God, sir?' said Toby.

Mr Tomlinson grunted, but said nothing.

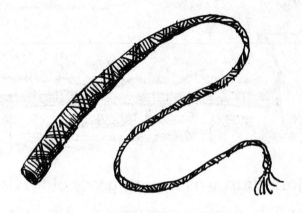

3

A Slave's Life

It took many weeks for Jonathan Strong to recover from his injuries. Mr Tomlinson and Toby visited him regularly. At first, Jonathan was too weak to say much, but as his health slowly improved, he began to tell his story.

Jonathan was twenty years old. His parents had been captured in Africa by slave-traders, packed into the dark, filthy hold of a ship and taken to the island of Barbados in the West Indies.

When their son
was born, they
called him
Olauda, but
slaves were
not allowed
to name their
children. The
owner of the
sugar plantation
called the baby
Jonathan Strong.
Jonathan started
work almost
as soon as he
could walk.

The slaves
were treated cruelly.
They worked from dawn to sundown in
the tropical heat, tending and harvesting

fields of sugar cane, or in the steamy
sheds where the sugar was boiled. Their
overseers carried whips, and often beat the
slaves for working too slowly. Anyone who
dared to answer an overseer back was
stripped to the waist, tied to a wooden
frame and lashed.

When Jonathan was eight, his father
was sold to another plantation-owner,
and Jonathan never saw him again.
His mother died of fever when he was ten.

At the age of eighteen, Jonathan was
sold to David Lisle, a lawyer from
London. Lisle wanted a black servant

because they were fashionable. Jonathan was brought to London where he was taught to read and write, and how to behave in front of fine ladies and gentlemen. He found it difficult – there were so many strange things to remember. London was crowded, dark and cold. Jonathan caught many chills, and he was clumsy when he served people.

Lisle had a quick temper, and often beat Jonathan with a riding crop.

Then one day Lisle became so enraged that he used a pistol to strike Jonathan over and over again. The blows were so violent that the pistol broke into pieces. Lisle could see that Jonathan was badly hurt, but he ordered him to be thrown out of the house. Two servants had carried him away and left him in a quiet back-street, thinking that he was sure to die.

Toby was shocked by what he heard.

He had known that slaves had a hard life, but people always talked about them as if they were more like animals than human beings. Jonathan was the first slave he had ever met, and Toby liked him. He was intelligent and quick to laugh, in spite of all that had happened to him.

'He's got the same feelings as anyone else,' thought Toby. 'How can it be right for someone to treat him the way that he's been treated?'

He asked Mr Tomlinson about it as they were walking back from the hospital one evening, and Mr Tomlinson's answer was short. 'Because slavery makes people rich,' he said.

'How?' said Toby.

'Merchants buy goods from English factories,' said Mr Tomlinson. 'There's profit for the factory-owners. The goods

are shipped to Africa and exchanged for
slaves. There's profit for the slave-traders.
The slaves are shipped to sugar
plantations in the West Indies, and cotton
plantations in America, and sold.
There's profit for the slave-auctioneers.
The merchants use the money from selling
slaves to buy cotton, sugar and spices,
which are brought back to England
for sale.

There's profit for the merchants. When fine ladies sweeten their coffee or tea with sugar, they do not think of the slaves who worked to grow it. When gentlemen dress in cotton shirts, they do not think of the slaves working on the plantations.'

'Does nobody care about the slaves, sir?' said Toby.

'Many people do,' Mr Tomlinson told him. 'Men like Thomas Clarkson and William Wilberforce have sworn to bring slavery to an end, but many rich and powerful people are against them. It will be a long struggle.'

'I wish I could help them!' said Toby.

'It is not in our power to abolish slavery, Toby,' said Mr Tomlinson. 'But I think I may be able to do something for Jonathan. Mr Carter, a friend of mine, is looking for a new servant. I shall mention Jonathan's name to him.'

And so it was that two months later, Jonathan Strong was employed by Mr Carter and began a new life.

But the shadow of his old life was to fall over him once again, and threaten his freedom.

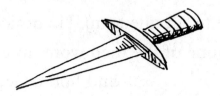

4

Kidnap

In the months that followed, Mr Carter
made regular visits to Pickett Place, and
always brought Jonathan with him.
Jonathan was troubled with headaches and
chest-pains as a result of his beating, but
otherwise he was happy. Mr Carter was a

considerate master, and treated him well.

One morning, Mr Carter sent Jonathan to deliver a letter to one of his business partners. On his way back, Jonathan saw two men chatting near the entrance to an alleyway. He noticed them because one of the men wore an eye-patch and had a deep scar on his left cheek.

As Jonathan was passing, the men suddenly grabbed him and bundled him into the alley. The man with the eye-patch pinned Jonathan's hands behind him, and the other drew a knife.

'What do you want with me?' Jonathan cried.

A third man emerged from a doorway, where he had been hiding. He had a round, plump face and his lips were twisted into a cruel smile.

Jonathan recognised him at once. 'Mr Lisle!' he gasped.

'You seem to have made a remarkable recovery, Jonathan,' Mr Lisle said. 'When I first saw you in the street three weeks ago, I could hardly believe my eyes. I followed you, made enquiries and then made arrangements.'

'Please let me go, sir!' Jonathan

pleaded. 'I work for Mr Carter now!'

'Nonsense!' Mr Lisle snapped. 'You are a runaway slave and you belong to me. Or rather, you once belonged to me. I have sold you to Mr James Kerr, and you will sail on tomorrow morning's tide to work on his plantation in Jamaica. My carriage is waiting to take you to the docks.' He glanced at the two men. 'Bring him!'

The man holding Jonathan's arms pushed him forward while the other brought the point of his knife up to Jonathan's throat. 'Easy, boy!' the man with the knife said. 'Not a word.'

That afternoon, Mr Tomlinson was surprised when a rough-looking sailor entered his shop.

'Are you Mr Tomlinson?' the sailor asked.

'I am. How may I help you?' said Mr Tomlinson.

The sailor reached into the pocket of his breeches and brought out a piece of folded paper. 'A man paid me to bring you this letter,' he said.

'What man?' Mr Tomlinson demanded.

The sailor seemed uneasy. 'All I know is I was paid to bring you this letter, and I have, and that's my part done!' he said. He thrust the letter into Mr Tomlinson's hand and hurried out of the shop.

The letter was from Jonathan, and it explained what had happened to him. He was on board a ship called *The Mirabelle*, which was setting sail for Jamaica the following morning.

'Toby!' Mr Tomlinson called out.

Toby appeared from a back room. 'What is it, sir?' he said.

'Jonathan has been taken by slave hunters and is a prisoner aboard ship,' said Mr Tomlinson. 'Tell George to shut up the shop, then come with me.'

'Where are we going, sir?' said Toby.

'To the magistrate's court,' Mr Tomlinson declared. 'I shall take out a writ to stop the ship from sailing until Jonathan is freed.'

It was seven o' clock when
Mr Tomlinson arrived at the dock where
The Mirabelle was moored. With him
were Toby, and two Bow Street Runners.
The captain refused to let them on board
at first, but he soon changed his mind
when he saw the writ.

'You are holding a free man against
his will,' Mr Tomlinson said.

'I was told he was a runaway slave,'
the captain protested.

'I do not care what you were told,'
Mr Tomlinson said sternly. 'Release the
man at once, or you will be arrested for
kidnapping.'

The captain reluctantly ordered one of
his crew to fetch Jonathan, who burst into
tears when he saw Mr Tomlinson and Toby.

'How can I ever repay you for what you have done, sir?' he sobbed.

'It is not over yet, Jonathan,' said Mr Tomlinson. 'I think that Mr Lisle is not a man to give up easily. I fear that we have not heard the last of him.'

'He wouldn't try to snatch Jonathan again, would he, sir?' said Toby.

'He is a lawyer,' Mr Tomlinson said.

At the time, Toby was not sure what Mr Tomlinson meant by this, but he was soon to find out.

5

A Trial

Jonathan stayed at Mr Tomlinson's house, too afraid to go out in case he was seized again. His headaches became worse, and he had nightmares about being back on the plantation where he had grown up.

A week after Jonathan had been freed,

Mr Tomlinson was served with a writ. He was charged with stealing Jonathan from his rightful owner, Mr Lisle, and would have to stand trial. Mr Tomlinson went immediately to see his lawyers, and when he returned he seemed depressed. 'The case is to be tried before Lord Mansfield, the Lord Chief Justice,' he told Toby and Jonathan.

'Is that a good thing?' Jonathan said.

'Hardly, he is a slave-owner himself,' said Mr Tomlinson. 'Mr Lisle is cunning. No doubt he will fill the public gallery with his supporters.'

Toby thought for a second, then said, 'If so many people are against slavery, couldn't you let them know about the trial, Mr Tomlinson? It might help to show the judge that you've got people on your side.'

Mr Tomlinson's eyes lit up. 'An excellent idea!' he exclaimed. 'I shall write a letter to the British Society for the Abolition of Slavery at once!'

'I will never be a slave again!' Jonathan vowed. 'I will hang myself first!'

'We must pray that it does not come to that,' said Mr Tomlinson. 'Our best hope lies with the jury. Lord Mansfield may be a slave-owner, but he is not the one who will decide the outcome of the case.'

Mr Tomlinson spoke reassuringly, but deep inside he knew that the chances of success were slim.

The trial lasted for two days. The public gallery was packed with members of the British Society for the Abolition of Slavery, who were so noisy that more than once Lord Mansfield threatened to clear the court.

However, there was a deadly hush
when Mr Lisle stepped
into the witness box.
He was sure that he
would win, and he
answered questions
with a smug grin.

When Mr Tomlinson's lawyer asked him
why he had beaten Jonathan and had him
thrown into the street, Mr Lisle said, 'He
was a useless piece of property. When I
saw him in the street some months later,
fit and well, I decided to sell him.
Everything I have done is perfectly legal,

and you cannot prove otherwise.'

Mr Tomlinson gave his evidence in a loud, clear voice. 'I stole nothing from Mr Lisle,' he said. 'I do not regard Jonathan Strong as property, but as a man. Mr Lisle knows the law better than I do, but I think that I understand justice, and he has behaved unjustly.'

Just before the members of the jury retired to decide their verdict, Lord

Mansfield spoke to them. 'Think carefully,' he said. 'For the real question at the heart of this case is whether slavery is legal in Britain or not.'

The jury were gone for a long time. Toby, who was in the public gallery with Jonathan, could hardly bear the waiting. Jonathan sat with his head in his hands, praying silently.

At last, someone whispered, 'Here they come!' and the jury filed back into the jury box.

'Have you reached a verdict?' Lord Mansfield demanded.

'We have, my lord,' replied the foreman of the jury. 'We find Mr Tomlinson not guilty of theft. Jonathan Strong is a free man who should never have been kidnapped.'

There was an uproar. People in the
gallery cheered, and began to chant, 'No
property! No property!'

'You're free!' Toby said to Jonathan.

Jonathan was laughing and crying at
the same time. 'Free?' he said above the
noise. 'What does that mean, Toby?'

'It means nobody owns you,' said Toby. 'You can't be bought and sold any more.'

Toby was glad for his friend, proud of Mr Tomlinson and proud of himself too. 'If I hadn't taken that short-cut...' he thought, but the thought was interrupted by the cheering of the crowd.

Notes

This story is based upon events
that happened in London.
Jonathan Strong lived as
a free man, but never fully
recovered from the beating that
David Lisle had given to him, and
died when he was 25.

Though slavery was outlawed in Britain, the slave
trade remained legal until it was banned by an Act
of Parliament in 1807. The main centres of the
slave trade were the ports of Bristol and Liverpool.
Between 1760 and 1810, British ships carried more
than 1,600,000 slaves from Africa to the West
Indies and America.

Conditions on board the slave ships were poor. The male slaves were shackled together in the hold, where it was dark, and only allowed out once a day to take exercise. No one knows how many died from disease. It was common for slaves to jump overboard, preferring to drown rather than face slavery.

Slavery remained legal in the British Colonies until 1833, when the Emancipation Act was passed. In America, slavery was legal until 1863, and was one of the major causes of the American Civil War (1861-1865).

In Parliament, the great champion of freedom for slaves was William Wilberforce (1750 - 1830), MP for Yorkshire. He was a deeply religious man who won many people over with his skill as a public speaker.

Thomas Clarkson (1760 - 1846) was one of the driving forces of the anti-slavery movement. He did research into the slave trade and did all he could to let the public know what he had discovered. He persuaded the owner of the Wedgewood factory to produce a plate, on which was a picture of a slave in chains, and the words, 'Am I not a man, and a brother?'. Thousands of

people bought copies of the plate to show their support.
A memorial plaque honouring Thomas Clarkson was unveiled in Westminster Abbey in 1996.

Anti-Slavery International was founded in 1839.
Its first President was Thomas Clarkson.
It still exists today, protecting the rights of poor, exploited people throughout the world.

Sparks: Historical Adventures

ANCIENT GREECE
The Great Horse of Troy – The Trojan War
0 7496 3369 7 (hbk)   0 7496 3538 X (pbk)
The Winner's Wreath – Ancient Greek Olympics
0 7496 3368 9 (hbk)   0 7496 3555 X (pbk)

INVADERS AND SETTLERS
Boudicca Strikes Back – The Romans in Britain
0 7496 3366 2 (hbk)   0 7496 3546 0 (pbk)
Viking Raiders – A Norse Attack
0 7496 3089 2 (hbk)   0 7496 3457 X (pbk)
Erik's New Home – A Viking Town
0 7496 3367 0 (hbk)   0 7496 3552 5 (pbk)
TALES OF THE ROWDY ROMANS
The Great Necklace Hunt
0 7496 2221 0 (hbk)   0 7496 2628 3 (pbk)
The Lost Legionary
0 7496 2222 9 (hbk)   0 7496 2629 1 (pbk)
The Guard Dog Geese
0 7496 2331 4 (hbk)   0 7496 2630 5 (pbk)
A Runaway Donkey
0 7496 2332 2 (hbk)   0 7496 2631 3 (pbk)

TUDORS AND STUARTS
Captain Drake's Orders – The Armada
0 7496 2556 2 (hbk)   0 7496 3121 X (pbk)
London's Burning – The Great Fire of London
0 7496 2557 0 (hbk)   0 7496 3122 8 (pbk)
Mystery at the Globe – Shakespeare's Theatre
0 7496 3096 5 (hbk)   0 7496 3449 9 (pbk)
Plague! – A Tudor Epidemic
0 7496 3365 4 (hbk)   0 7496 3556 8 (pbk)
Stranger in the Glen – Rob Roy
0 7496 2586 4 (hbk)   0 7496 3123 6 (pbk)
A Dream of Danger – The Massacre of Glencoe
0 7496 2587 2 (hbk)   0 7496 3124 4 (pbk)
A Queen's Promise – Mary Queen of Scots
0 7496 2589 9 (hbk)   0 7496 3125 2 (pbk)
Over the Sea to Skye – Bonnie Prince Charlie
0 7496 2588 0 (hbk)   0 7496 3126 0 (pbk)
TALES OF A TUDOR TEARAWAY
A Pig Called Henry
0 7496 2204 4 (hbk)   0 7496 2625 9 (pbk)
A Horse Called Deathblow
0 7496 2205 9 (hbk)   0 7496 2624 0 (pbk)
Dancing for Captain Drake
0 7496 2234 2 (hbk)   0 7496 2626 7 (pbk)
Birthdays are a Serious Business
0 7496 2235 0 (hbk)   0 7496 2627 5 (pbk)

VICTORIAN ERA
The Runaway Slave – The British Slave Trade
0 7496 3093 0 (hbk)   0 7496 3456 1 (pbk)
The Sewer Sleuth – Victorian Cholera
0 7496 2590 2 (hbk)   0 7496 3128 7 (pbk)
Convict! – Criminals Sent to Australia
0 7496 2591 0 (hbk)   0 7496 3129 5 (pbk)
An Indian Adventure – Victorian India
0 7496 3090 6 (hbk)   0 7496 3451 0 (pbk)
Farewell to Ireland – Emigration to America
0 7496 3094 9 (hbk)   0 7496 3448 0 (pbk)

The Great Hunger – Famine in Ireland
0 7496 3095 7 (hbk)   0 7496 3447 2 (pbk)
Fire Down the Pit – A Welsh Mining Disaster
0 7496 3091 4 (hbk)   0 7496 3450 2 (pbk)
Tunnel Rescue – The Great Western Railway
0 7496 3353 0 (hbk)   0 7496 3537 1 (pbk)
Kidnap on the Canal – Victorian Waterways
0 7496 3352 2 (hbk)   0 7496 3540 1 (pbk)
Dr. Barnardo's Boys – Victorian Charity
0 7496 3358 1 (hbk)   0 7496 3541 X (pbk)
The Iron Ship – Brunel's Great Britain
0 7496 3355 7 (hbk)   0 7496 3543 6 (pbk)
Bodies for Sale – Victorian Tomb-Robbers
0 7496 3364 6 (hbk)   0 7496 3539 8 (pbk)
Penny Post Boy – The Victorian Postal Service
0 7496 3362 X (hbk)   0 7496 3544 4 (pbk)
The Canal Diggers – The Manchester Ship Canal
0 7496 3356 5 (hbk)   0 7496 3545 2 (pbk)
The Tay Bridge Tragedy – A Victorian Disaster
0 7496 3354 9 (hbk)   0 7496 3547 9 (pbk)
Stop, Thief! – The Victorian Police
0 7496 3359 X (hbk)   0 7496 3548 7 (pbk)
Miss Buss and Miss Beale – Victorian Schools
0 7496 3360 3 (hbk)   0 7496 3549 5 (pbk)
Chimney Charlie – Victorian Chimney Sweeps
0 7496 3351 4 (hbk)   0 7496 3551 7 (pbk)
Down the Drain – Victorian Sewers
0 7496 3357 3 (hbk)   0 7496 3550 9 (pbk)
The Ideal Home – A Victorian New Town
0 7496 3361 1 (hbk)   0 7496 3553 3 (pbk)
Stage Struck – Victorian Music Hall
0 7496 3367 0 (hbk)   0 7496 3554 1 (pbk)
TRAVELS OF A YOUNG VICTORIAN
The Golden Key
0 7496 2360 8 (hbk)   0 7496 2632 1 (pbk)
Poppy's Big Push
0 7496 2361 6 (hbk)   0 7496 2633 X (pbk)
Poppy's Secret
0 7496 2374 8 (hbk)   0 7496 2634 8 (pbk)
The Lost Treasure
0 7496 2375 6 (hbk)   0 7496 2635 6 (pbk)

20th-CENTURY HISTORY
Fight for the Vote – The Suffragettes
0 7496 3092 2 (hbk)   0 7496 3452 9 (pbk)
The Road to London – The Jarrow March
0 7496 2609 7 (hbk)   0 7496 3132 5 (pbk)
The Sandbag Secret – The Blitz
0 7496 2608 9 (hbk)   0 7496 3133 3 (pbk)
Sid's War – Evacuation
0 7496 3209 7 (hbk)   0 7496 3445 6 (pbk)
D-Day! – Wartime Adventure
0 7496 3208 9 (hbk)   0 7496 3446 4 (pbk)
The Prisoner – A Prisoner of War
0 7496 3212 7 (hbk)   0 7496 3455 3 (pbk)
Escape from Germany – Wartime Refugees
0 7496 3211 9 (hbk)   0 7496 3454 5 (pbk)
Flying Bombs – Wartime Bomb Disposal
0 7496 3210 0 (hbk)   0 7496 3453 7 (pbk)
12,000 Miles From Home – Sent to Australia
0 7496 3370 0 (hbk)   0 7496 3542 8 (pbk)